Happy Birthday, Pooh!

Bruce Talkington
ILLUSTRATED BY John Kurtz

New York

Printed in the United States of America.

The type for this book was set in 15-point Cochin.

The artwork for each picture was prepared using watercolor and pencil.

Based on the Pooh stories by A. A. Milne (copyright The Pooh Properties Trust).

First Edition
1 3 5 7 9 10 8 6 4 2

Library of Congress Catalog Card Number: 98-86430
ISBN: 0-7868-3218-5

For more Disney Press fun, visit www.disneybooks.com

Happy Birthday, Pooh!

Spring was a busy time for Piglet. There always seemed to be another thing that needed doing.

In the midst of all this activity, Piglet was certain that he'd forgotten something very important!

Had he forgotten to water the rhododendrons? No. Had he forgotten to polish his tea things? No. And just as he was wondering if he had forgotten to wax the floors, his feet slid out from under him and he sledded across the room.

"No," he sighed, "that isn't it, either."

"What I've forgotten must be very important," said Piglet. "And what could be more important than Winnie the Pooh's birthday?

"Poor Pooh Bear," said Piglet with a sad sigh. "But the day is not over yet! Rabbit will help me plan Pooh's party."

Piglet ran out of his house and down the path toward Rabbit's.

Rabbit was busy inspecting his tomatoes. "If these tomatoes were any greener and any smaller," he grumbled, "they'd be olives! What could possibly be worse than this!"

Suddenly Tigger came out of the sky and bounced Rabbit with a mighty "Hoo-hoo-HOO!" Piglet arrived at that same moment and found himself squished beneath his two friends.

"Sorry," apologized Tigger. "I was tryin' for a really bouncidy bounce an' you two got in the way."

Piglet told Rabbit and Tigger that it must be Pooh's birthday. "I wouldn't have forgotten to remember it if it weren't," he explained.

Rabbit and Tigger agreed that it certainly sounded as if it must be today.

"We have to organize a party immediately," announced Rabbit.

"We need a birthday cake," said Tigger.

"And a few balloons," suggested Piglet.

"An' a birthday cake," Tigger said again, almost shouting.

"And, of course, we'll need a birthday cake," Rabbit declared.

"Ooo, what a splendiferous idea," hooted Tigger excitedly. "Why didn't I think o' that?"

"I'll bring the candles!" shouted the three friends at the same time, and off they scrambled in different directions!

Rabbit pulled out every candle he could carry. "I'd better take a few extra," he told himself. "Just to be on the safe side."

Piglet
filled his arms
with lots of
brightly colored
candles. "I'd
better take a
few extra," he
gasped. "Just to
be on the safe side."

Tigger
also grabbed a
box of candles.
"Better take a
few extra," he
said. "Just in—
well, there's
gotta be some
reason."

Pooh's birthday cake wound up with so many candles that it was almost impossible to see any cake!

"Why," declared Rabbit, "with all these candles it appears our friend Pooh is much older than we thought."

"Oh, my," said Piglet. "If Pooh's that much older than we thought, isn't he that much smarter as well?"

"Now, now," blurted Rabbit, "let's not jump to conclusions."

"Let's jump over to Pooh Boy's house an' tell 'im what a genius he is!" suggested Tigger. "He'll never figure it out on his own."

Rabbit, Tigger, and Piglet took the cake over to Pooh's house. "Surprise!" they yelled as he opened the door.

"Oh," responded Pooh. "I thought it was a birthday cake."

"See?" said Tigger. "I told ya he was smart!"

"Just look at all the candles, Pooh," Piglet pointed out. "You're so very much older than we thought."

"And very much brighter, too," sniffed Rabbit doubtfully.

"It's the candles that are bright," laughed Pooh, "not me."

"There's just no foolin' this guy," chuckled Tigger.

A familiar rumbling sounded from Pooh's middle. "Perhaps," he suggested, "we can discuss this further over a not-so-very-small smackerel of cake?"

As they all sat watching Pooh blow out the candles one by one, Rabbit decided to see just how smart his friend was. "Pooh Bear," he asked, "what am I to do about my tomatoes?"

"Well, I suppose that would depend on how the tomatoes feel. Wouldn't it?" Pooh replied.

Rabbit's ears perked straight up. "Why, yes," he answered. "It very much would." Rabbit hurried away to put Pooh's advice to work.

"Hey, Pooh Boy, what's the best way for me to cover more ground with my bouncifryin'?" Tigger asked.

"When you bounce up, just don't come back down," said Pooh.

"Whaddaya know," gasped Tigger in awe. "Buddy Bear really is ingenerous!"

He bounced away, trying to stay in the air longer with each leap.

Finally, Piglet asked politely, "Pooh, how long shall I take with my spring cleaning?"

Pooh, licking frosting off his paw, answered, "Spring? Well, there does seem to be a very great deal of it outside, Piglet."

"Clean ALL of spring?" squeaked Piglet. "Oh d-d-dear."

Pooh finally blew out the last candle.

"Now for some cake," he announced happily. But his smile disappeared when he saw that he was all alone.

"Well," he sighed as he tucked the candles into an empty honeypot, "I'll save the candles for later. Just to be on the safe side."

Then he tasted the cake and thought how much his friends would enjoy it when they got back from wherever they'd gone.

Later that day, Owl was flying over Rabbit's garden when he heard a voice.

"The only way I can know how a tomato feels," it said, "is to feel like a tomato."

Below him, Owl saw a huge tomato with a familiar pair of long ears poking out of the top. "A talking tomato?" he asked.

"No, it's me," replied Rabbit. "I need to get to know my vegetables. It's Pooh's idea. He's much smarter than we thought!"

"Did you hear that?" Rabbit asked, standing very still.

Rabbit scurried off through the rows of vegetables. "Stop! Don't start talking until I get there!"

Owl continued through the Hundred-Acre Wood until he heard a shout. "Look out beloooooooow!"

A moment later, Tigger landed at his feet with a loud THUMP!

"Tigger," asked Owl, "are you all right?"

"This not comin' down stuff is trickier than it looks," moaned Tigger. "Hoo-hoo-Oooo, that smarts."

Tigger climbed painfully to his feet. "But Buddy Bear told me
I could do it, so I'm gonna. That fluff he thinks with has gotten
awful smart, ya know." Tigger exited with a mighty bounce.

"I'd better get to the bottom of this," Owl declared, "before
Tigger breaks his. Bottom, that is."

As Owl neared Pooh's house, he saw Piglet scurrying down the path, sweeping under rocks and thumbtacking fallen leaves back onto the trees.

"Piglet," questioned Owl, "what are you doing?"

"Spring cleaning," said Piglet, as he lifted a fish from a nearby pond and dusted it.

"But doesn't that take place inside?" Owl asked.

"Not according to Pooh," answered Piglet. "And he's a bear of very large brain, you know."

"No, I don't know," said Owl. "But I'm going to find out!"

Owl sat across the table from Pooh. Between them was one small piece of cake with a single candle.

"Would you care for a piece of my oh-what-a-surprise birthday cake?" Pooh asked politely.

"Thank you, Pooh Bear," answered Owl, "but first I'd like to ask you a question."

"I love questions," said Pooh, "as long as no one cares too much what the answer is."

"If I have five pots of honey," began Owl, "and I take away three of them, how many pots of honey do I have left?"

"Not enough for breakfast, I'm afraid," Pooh answered sadly.

Owl's beak dropped open. Was Pooh smarter than he thought?

Pooh and Owl looked up as Tigger and Piglet pushed Rabbit through the front door.

"Hello!" exclaimed Pooh happily. "You're just in time for something. I'm sure I'll remember what in a moment."

"Pooh Bear," began Piglet nervously, "we're just a bit concerned that the wise advice you gave us may not have been so very wise after all."

"Oh, I remember," interrupted Pooh. "There's still enough for all of us to have a smackerel or two of cake."

"One candle?" blurted Tigger.

"This means Pooh isn't as old or as smart as we thought he was," burst out Rabbit.

"Oh, Pooh!" cried Piglet, delighted. "You really are the bear we thought you were."

"Thank you," said Pooh, though he wasn't at all certain what he was thanking Piglet for. "Now that that's settled, do you think we can all enjoy this birthday . . . slice?"

"Pooh Bear," hooted Tigger, "that's a terrifical smart idea."